Facing Our Energy Problem

THE HEAT IS ON

By Shelley Tanaka

Illustrated by Steve Beinicke

LIBRARY
Antioch New England Graduate School
40 Avon St
Keene NH 03431-3516

**earth
care
books**

FIREFLY BOOKS

TJ163.35.T35 1991

Text copyright © 1991 by Shelley Tanaka
Illustrations copyright © 1991 by Steve Beinicke

All rights reserved. No part of this book may be reproduced or transmitted in any form by any means without permission in writing from the publisher, except by a reviewer, who may quote brief passages in a review.

First published in Canada by
Douglas & McIntyre Ltd.

Published in the United States in 1991 by
Firefly Books (U.S.) Inc.
P.O. Box 1325
Ellicott Station
Buffalo, New York 14205

Canadian Cataloguing in Publication Data

Tanaka, Shelley
    The heat is on

(Earthcare books)
ISBN 0-920668-94-1

1. Energy conservation—Juvenile literature.
2. Power resources—Juvenile literature.
I. Beinicke, Steven, 1956–   . II. Title.
III. Series.

TJ163.35.T35 1991   j333.791'6   C91-094274-9

Special thanks to Sheila Malcolmson, Energy Probe, Toronto, and Dr. Steve Harrison, Department of Mechanical Engineering, Queen's University, Kingston, for their helpful comments on the manuscript; and to Bob Richardson, Nelson High School, Burlington, Ontario, for the sidebar information on page 52.

Design by Michael Solomon
Printed and bound in Hong Kong

Contents

PART 1: What Is Energy, and Why Do We Use So Much of It? / 5

PART 2: Where Does Energy Come From? / 12
    Fossil Fuels / 14
    Water Power / 26
    Nuclear Power / 30
    Other Sources of Energy / 36

PART 3: What Can We Do? / 42

    Glossary / 54
    Index / 56

PART 1

What Is Energy, and Why Do We Use So Much of It?

"Energy" is what makes things go. Everything that moves or runs or pumps or beams uses some kind of energy. This energy might come from your body's muscles when you push the pedals to make your bike go. Or it might come from the heat of burning coal. A machine called a generator can change this heat into the electricity that comes into your house to make your appliances and lights work.

Energy heats your house and your school. It makes your TV go on, gets you from place to place and powers the factories and machines that make the hundreds of things you use every day, from your toothbrush to your sneakers and video games. From the moment you wake up in the morning to the sound of the clock radio to the time you turn off the lights before you go to bed at night, you use energy.

Lots and lots of energy.

TIMES HAVE CHANGED! OUR

We haven't always used so much energy. Only one hundred years ago, perhaps when your great-great-grandparents were growing up, life was quite different.

In fact, a typical winter day might have gone something like this:

5:30 a.m. Hear early-morning sounds of father down in kitchen, throwing more wood into stove (only source of heat in house).

6:30 a.m. Get up when morning light streams through window. Your room is so cold that you can see your breath. Wooden floor feels freezing cold on your bare feet. Quickly put on several layers of clothing and go downstairs. Rush outside to outhouse to go to bathroom.

7:00 a.m. Porridge is bubbling on wood stove. Cut thick slice of bread and clamp between two wire racks. Place over open stove top to make toast. Get butter out of ice box. Fetch potatoes, squash, carrots and onions from cellar and cut up for stew for dinner, which will sit cooking all day while warmth from stove heats house.

8:00 a.m. Gather up books and leave house for 45-minute walk to school.

9:00 a.m. Put container of milk in stream by school to keep cool. Help gather wood for stove that keeps schoolhouse warm.

6 / The Heat Is On

ENERGY NEEDS – THEN AND NOW

On the other hand, a typical kid's day today would be quite different:

8:00 a.m. Wake up to sound of clock radio. Check digital clock for time, press Doze button and go back to sleep for 10 minutes.

8:15 a.m. Have hot shower. Dry hair with blow-dryer. Sort through laundry in dryer for favorite T-shirt.

8:30 a.m. Listen to weather forecast on radio. Plug in kettle to boil water for instant hot chocolate. Make toast in automatic toaster. Grab Walkman and books and rush out door. Beg Mum for lift home since rain is predicted.

9:00 a.m. Arrive at school. Today's classes include computers, language lab and a film on windmills.

3:30 p.m. Mum waiting in car outside school, engine running. Drive ten blocks home. Stop off at mall on the way; play video game while Mum does insta-banking, picks up dry-cleaning and buys hamburger buns for dinner.

4:00 p.m. Grab snack out of fridge, phone best friend for chat. Play stereo while doing homework. Turn up volume when noise of vacuum cleaner in next room gets too loud.

What Is Energy? / 7

3:30 p.m. Walk home to do chores. Sweep floors. Chop wood for stove and bring into house. Take dry clothes off line and fold or iron, using iron heated on stove.

5:00 p.m. Light oil lamps as it begins to get dark. Eat dinner while discussing chores to be done next day.

5:30 p.m. Pour hot water from pot on stove into dishpan. Wash dishes by hand and dry them with dishcloth. Cover bowl of leftover food with tea towel and place in unheated room next to kitchen to keep cool.

7:00 p.m. Do homework by light of oil lamp. Get out skates and polish so they will be ready when pond freezes over after Christmas. Do hand mending. Write letters. Fill hot-water bottle with hot water and run upstairs to put under covers to warm bed. Hurry back down to warm kitchen.

8:30 p.m. Eyes getting sore from reading in dim light. Go upstairs and quickly get into bed. Sounds drift up through hole in floor that lets heat rise up from kitchen into your room. Fall asleep to sounds of parents putting more wood into stove for the night before they go to bed, too.

8 / The Heat Is On

6:00 p.m. Go into kitchen to help prepare dinner. Defrost meat in microwave. Chop onions in food processor for hamburgers, take frozen French fries out of freezer, preheat broiler in oven, switch on automatic coffeemaker.

6:30 p.m. Eat dinner while listening to evening news on radio.

7:00 p.m. Put dishes in dishwasher. Cover leftover food with plastic wrap and put in refrigerator.

7:15 p.m. Get ride to hockey practice. Hang out with friends while Zamboni clears artificial ice. Get cold drink from pop machine.

8:30 p.m. Home from practice, watch movie on VCR. Turn up heat a bit since house seems kind of chilly.

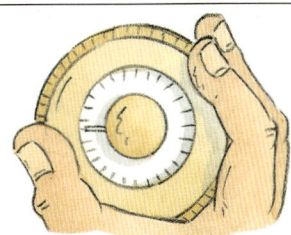

10:30 p.m. Listen to Walkman in bed before turning off light. Fall asleep listening to hum of fridge, occasional clunk of electric furnace going on, and faint noises from TV still on in living room.

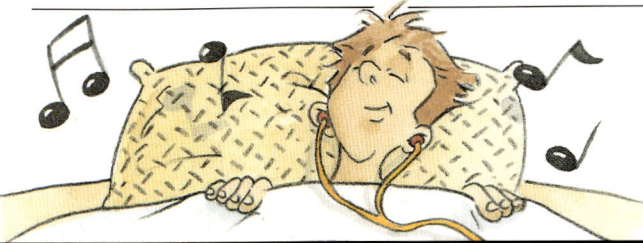

What Is Energy? / **9**

Did You Know?

Turning off a typical desktop computer, monitor and printer on nights and weekends for six years will lower your electricity bill enough to pay for the whole system!

It's pretty clear that we use more energy today than we did one hundred years ago. We are constantly inventing new machines to do our work for us so we can cook our meals more quickly, type up our projects more easily, dial our phones in seconds. We are hopping into our cars more and more, to pick up a video or a case of pop, or to get us to another lesson or game or meeting. We are using enormous amounts of energy to keep our houses and shopping malls heated in the winter and cool in the summer.

But we also use a lot more energy because we have more things—not just machines and appliances, but everything from fluorescent pens and binders to sports equipment and magazines. All these things use energy—to run the machines that make them and package them, and to fuel the trucks that transport them to the stores.

We love our things. They entertain us and make our lives easier. We can't wait to replace them with a bigger house, a car with more power, a better computer game, a stronger air-conditioner, a wider TV screen, a fancier phone, a bigger fridge.

This means we will use even more energy in the years to come.

Remember the Blackout?

Have you ever had a power blackout? If you were at school when it happened, you were probably dismissed early, because there were no lights in the halls, classrooms or washrooms, and no heat in the building. Maybe your parents came home from work early, too, because none of the computers or phones were working in the office, and no machinery was running. (Maybe they complained about having to walk down hundreds of stairs, because the office elevators weren't working!)

If you were at home, you probably found that things suddenly became creepy and quiet—no radio or TV noises, no fridge or furnace humming. Perhaps you ate a peanut butter sandwich for dinner, because the stove couldn't be turned on, and maybe you noticed that the milk in the refrigerator was starting to get a little warm.

If it was after dark, it probably felt strange not being able to watch television or play a video game or listen to the stereo. Outside, the streetlights were out, and all the houses on your street were dark. Maybe you tried to read by candlelight until your eyes got a bit sore from the dim light. Or perhaps you put on an extra sweatshirt or socks because the house was starting to get chilly.

Maybe you even went to bed early, because you figured there was nothing else to do!

Sometimes it takes a power blackout to make us realize how much we depend on energy, and how much energy we use just getting through a regular day.

But now we have an energy problem. We are using up all the energy supplies we have, and we don't have new, safe sources to take their place. What is even worse, our enormous consumption of energy is destroying the earth. In fact, the production of energy probably causes more pollution than any other human activity.

We can't go on like this. We must start using our energy sources wisely and carefully. More important, we must start really thinking about where our energy comes from and why using so much of it is damaging our planet in a big way.

Did You Know?
■ If your television has remote control, electronic tuning and "instant-on" buttons, the TV is using energy even while the set is turned off. In the United States, these televisions consume the same amount of power that it would take to supply heat and electricity to over 50,000 homes.

■ Canadians are the world's biggest energy pigs. Each Canadian uses twice as much energy as a person in Japan or Sweden, and three times as much energy as a person in Denmark. Americans are the second biggest energy consumers.

PART 2

Where Does Energy Come From?

There are many sources of energy. Running water is a source of energy, and so are the sun and the wind. Fuels like oil, natural gas or wood can be burned in a furnace to heat our homes. Oil can also be turned into gasoline and burned in automobile engines to make cars run.

Or, these fuels can be turned into electricity—the electricity that comes out of the wall to make our lights and televisions and stoves work.

Turning Energy Into Electricity

To make electricity, the source of energy must first run a turbine—a wheel-like machine with metal blades that spin very fast. Sometimes running water rushes over the blades to make them spin. But most of the time some sort of fuel—oil, coal, natural gas or uranium—is used to boil water. The boiling water makes steam, and this steam pushes against the turbine blades to make them spin.

The turbine is attached to a generator—a machine that makes electricity. The spinning movement of the turbine blades whirls metal wires around powerful magnets, creating an electric

Did You Know?

The average car tire contains almost 8 liters (2 gallons) of oil. Getting rid of old tires is a big problem, since tire dumps can be a huge fire hazard (there are as many as 2 billion scrap tires in North America today). Some people think these old tires should be used as fuel, providing they can be burned cleanly and safely.

current. This current can be passed through wires over long distances from power plants to houses and buildings.

Fossil Fuels

Much of our energy comes from burning oil, coal and natural gas. We call these fossil fuels because they are made out of ancient animals and plants.

Oil and natural gas are made from dead sea plants and animals that once lived along the coasts of ancient oceans. When layers of sand and mud covered them up and pressed down on top of them over millions of years, the bodies slowly turned into oil and gas.

Coal is made from ancient trees and swamp plants that have been covered up and crushed in the same way.

Oil, coal and natural gas lie deep under the earth. They have to be dug up or pumped out of the ground before they can be used.

One of our problems is that fossil fuels are becoming scarce. Oil, coal and natural gas may still be forming deep in the earth, but this is happening so slowly that it will be many millions of years before anyone can use them. Many experts say that by the time you are a grownup, oil will be very scarce, and by the time you are a grandparent the oil we know about will be completely gone. It will take longer for us to run out of coal and natural gas, but eventually they will be gone, too.

Yet many power plants use oil, natural gas and coal to make electricity. Many homes are heated with oil. And, of course, practically all the cars in the world run on gasoline, which comes from oil.

To feed all these cars, furnaces and power stations, some people think we must simply work harder to find more fossil fuels. Oil companies and some governments have decided we must find whatever oil is left in the earth and get to it, no matter where it is, and no matter how much it costs. To find more oil for us to buy, they are going deep into the northern wilderness to dig up oily sand and rock. Huge machines are then used to squeeze the oil out of this rock.

It is very expensive and awkward to get oil this way. Not only that, but enormous amounts of water are used to help remove the oil, and this polluted water must then be cleaned up.

There are also plans to drill under the ocean off the coast of North America, even though this will probably damage priceless fishing grounds as well as sea plants and animals. Some companies even want to look for oil in Antarctica, the world's last wild continent.

Finding more oil may give us a bit more time to develop other sources of energy, but it will not solve the energy problem. The fact is that most of the easy-to-get-at oil is almost gone and, sooner or later, even whatever oil is left in the earth will be used up. Besides, we need oil for things other than fuel. Oil is used to make plastic as well as a lot of medicines, dyes and chemicals that we use every day.

There are serious problems with all other fossil fuels, too—finding them, getting them out of the ground, transporting them to the people and factories that want to use them.

Coal is difficult and dangerous to mine. And, because it is bulky and must be carried from the mines to the power plants by trucks or trains (rather than through pipelines like oil and gas), it is expensive to transport and uses up lots of energy simply getting from one place to another.

Some people think we should be using natural gas to heat our homes, run our power stations and even fuel our cars. Burning natural gas doesn't put sulfur dioxide into the air, so it is not a major cause of acid rain, and cars that are powered by natural gas produce less smog-forming exhaust than cars that run on gasoline. But burning natural gas sends out methane, which is a much worse Greenhouse gas (see p. 20) than carbon dioxide.

Even if the earth was bursting with fossil fuels, using oil, natural gas and coal to fill our energy

Did You Know?
Some people are finding ways to make fuel out of sheep fat, peanut oil, cow manure and even crushed farm wastes such as sawdust, nut shells, olive pits and corncobs.

needs would not be the answer, because there is an even bigger problem. Simply by using these fuels, we are polluting our air and our water so badly that we may damage the earth beyond repair, even before all the oil, coal and natural gas are gone.

Burning fossil fuels pollutes the planet in many different ways:

Acid Rain
When coal and oil are burned in power plants, factories or cars, harmful invisible gases are carried into the air with the exhaust smoke. Two of these gases are sulfur dioxide and nitrogen oxide.

These gases can stay in the air for up to four days, and during this time, the wind can carry them huge distances. When the gases get mixed in with the water in the atmosphere, they become acidic, like lemon juice. The acid water gathers in clouds and falls to the earth as rain or snow.

This acid rain kills trees and plants. It sinks into the soil and fills up lakes, killing the fish. As the fish disappear, the birds and animals that feed on the fish go away. Even the mosquitoes and frogs die.

The acid also wears away at the rocks in lakes and the inside of plumbing pipes, causing poisonous metals to be absorbed by plants or get into our drinking water.

There are ways to help stop these gases from getting into the air. Engineers are working on new devices that will stop cars from putting out so much nitrogen oxide. Special contraptions called scrubbers can be attached to factories and power plants to remove most of the sulfur dioxide. Some

Did You Know?
If you leave a 100-watt electric light on twelve hours a day for a whole year, it will use enough electricity to burn almost 180 kg (400 lb) of coal. Burning this coal will release 450 kg (1,000 lb) of carbon dioxide and 3.5 kg (8 lb) of acid rain-causing gases into the air.

companies say it costs too much to install these scrubbers. Other companies have found ways to save the sulfur gases and sell them for other uses.

If governments insist that we stop putting acid gases into the air, companies will try harder to find smart ways to clean up their act without losing piles of money.

If enough people complain, governments will put more pressure on businesses to reduce the amount of acid rain-causing gases they are putting into the air. Write to your government leaders and ask them what they are doing to make industries reduce acid rain. Find out which companies in your area produce the most acid emissions and write to ask them why they are doing this, and how they plan to fix it.

Where Does Energy Come From?

Greenhouse Effect

When coal, natural gas or oil are burned, they release carbon into the air, producing carbon dioxide gas. Carbon dioxide is a natural part of the atmosphere. We produce it every time we breathe, for instance, and plants and trees naturally soak it up. But if there is too much carbon dioxide, it collects like a blanket over the earth and acts like the glass on a greenhouse, trapping the sun's heat so the earth's atmosphere heats up.

Our cars and factories and power plants (especially the ones fueled by coal) are now creating so much carbon dioxide that many scientists believe this Greenhouse Effect is changing the earth's climate, making it warmer. So far, this is happening very gradually, but if we keep burning fossil fuels, our farmlands could become too dry or hot to grow crops. Rainfall and weather patterns may change, and the huge ice fields at the north and south poles may melt, causing the oceans to rise, and flooding seaside cities and lands.

Oil Spills

After oil has been pumped out of the ground, it is often carried by ship across the ocean to the places where it will be used. These huge supertankers—ships as long as four football fields—are extremely slow and difficult to maneuver, which means that it can take almost a half hour to bring a full one to a stop.

When a supertanker accidentally runs into an iceberg or rock, the ship's huge load of oil can spill out. There have been a number of accidents like this, but one of the worst ones occurred in 1989. That spring, the supertanker *Exxon Valdez* hit a rock off the coast of Alaska, spilling 41 million liters (10 million gallons) of oil into the ocean. This oil swept over 5,000 kilometers (3,100 miles) of shoreline, and in some places was 1 meter (3 feet) thick. It killed fish, sea otters, seals, porpoises, whales, deer and bears, as well as thousands and thousands of birds, including more than 150 endangered bald eagles.

At least 11,000 people worked to clean up the spilled oil. The cleanup cost $1 billion, and every method possible was tried, from special chemicals dropped from planes to scrubbing the rocks with paper towels. Even so, less than one-quarter of the oil was recovered. The rest stayed in the water or was washed up onto the rocks and sand along the coast. It will be several years before we know how long it will take for the land and the wildlife to return to normal.

We don't seem to have learned much from this disaster. In the year following the *Exxon Valdez* accident there were still more than 100 oil spills throughout the world, totalling at least 105 million liters (28 million gallons) of oil.

Even the oil companies admit that no matter how much money we spend, it is impossible to clean up a big oil spill completely. Go to your local library and get the name and address of one of the big oil companies. Write and ask them how they plan to deal with the next big oil spill.

Where Does Energy Come From? / 21

Wood as Fuel

In countries that don't have other sources of energy, wood may be the only fuel that people can use easily. But wood is heavy and awkward to transport over long distances, and new trees must be planted, or else the wood will run out. And, if everybody burned wood, there could be a big pollution problem, too. Some people think that countries with large open areas could plant fast-growing trees just for fuel. The wood could be burned to produce gas, and this gas could be transported through underground pipelines to power stations.

Smog

Half the oil we use goes to fuel our cars, trucks and airplanes. When cars burn gasoline, they produce gases that contribute to the Greenhouse Effect and acid rain. Cars also release unburned gasoline into the air, and when the sun hits this gasoline, dangerous chemicals are produced that cause smog—polluted air that is bad for people, animals and plants.

Some experts say that breathing the air in a traffic-choked city is as bad for you as smoking two packs of cigarettes a day. Some large cities are becoming so polluted with car exhaust, they are thinking of banning gasoline-powered cars from their roads altogether.

PLANT A TREE

Trees can help you save energy. Evergreen trees planted on the north side of your house can help stop the winter winds from cooling your home, which means you need less fuel for heat. In the summer, trees on the south side can help keep your house cool.

Trees and plants also absorb carbon dioxide. All over the world people are cutting down large forests for fuel, wood or paper, or to clear land for factories and grazing animals. This means that there are fewer trees to absorb all the carbon dioxide that we are producing. So plant a tree—in your backyard or in your schoolground. Good for the birds and animals, good for the atmosphere, good for us.

WANTED: THE POLLUTION-FREE CAR

Have you ever wondered why we can't just invent a car that won't pollute the air?

In fact, for years engineers have been working on the electric car—a car that doesn't run on gasoline, is quiet, and doesn't send polluting exhaust out its tailpipe. There are also cars that run on natural gas, propane and methane (many taxi cabs, for example, run on propane).

But these gasoline-free cars have problems, too. Cars that use natural gas still pollute the environment to some extent, and there are not many gas stations around that are equipped to fill them. And so far engineers have not been able to invent a car battery that is light, that can go for long distances without being recharged, and that can go as fast as gasoline-fueled cars.

Some cities have such a big pollution problem that they are thinking of encouraging people to drive electric cars in town. Even though they go more slowly, electric cars would be just fine for driving to the store, to school or to work. The expressways would be quiet and not filled with the stink of car exhaust, and people would recharge their batteries by plugging them into electrical outlets at night, when less electricity is being used by homes and factories.

But electric cars have to get their electricity from somewhere, and this could mean that oil- or coal-fueled power plants would have to work even harder. Instead of coming out of your tailpipe, more polluting gases might be coming out the smokestack of your city's generating station. Or perhaps another nuclear power station would have to be built to provide enough electricity for all those battery-run cars.

So if we can't invent a car that doesn't harm the environment, what's the answer?

We must drive our cars less. We must tell our governments to put their money into public transportation—trains, subways and buses—and to discourage people from hopping into their cars without thinking. And every time we step into our own cars, whether they run on gasoline, natural gas, or batteries, we must think about the environmental cost. How much fuel are we using? How much pollution is each trip causing?

Ride Your Bike . . . or Walk

Perhaps the simplest and most useful thing anyone can do about the pollution and energy problem is to ride a bike or walk. Many of us have become so used to being driven wherever we want to go, we've forgotten how to use our legs—to walk, or to pedal. The next time you want to ask for a lift somewhere, think about taking your bike instead. Brush up on your safety rules, wear a helmet, and rig up a secure basket or holder for your stuff.

BE A TREE WATCHER

Choose a tree in your backyard, in your favorite park, or in your schoolground. Examine the tree closely. Are the leaves or needles turning yellow around the edges and dropping off, even in the middle of summer? Are the branches at the top of the tree bare or drooping? Is the bark splitting or peeling? (These could be signs of acid rain damage.) Write down what you notice. Perhaps you can compare your results with those of the other kids in your class. Make a chart of your observations and send them to the government official in charge of the environment, and to a local nature organization. If you can, save your results and compare them with your observations of the same tree the following summer.

LOVING OUR CARS MORE THAN THE EARTH

We love our cars. We especially love cars that are fast and powerful, with power windows and air-conditioning and automatic seat warmers and sophisticated stereo systems. We drive our cars whenever we can, and we buy new ones as soon as we can afford it.

But our cars eat up a lot of energy. North Americans, for example, buy more than 725 million liters (190 million gallons) of gasoline *every day*. There are at least 500 million vehicles in the world, many of them carrying one grownup to work or to the store, or driving one kid to school or to a game or meeting.

We *must* stop driving our cars so much. Cars pollute the air, help cause acid rain and the Greenhouse Effect. They use up enormous amounts of oil.

You may not be able to drive or buy a car yet, but there are lots of things you can do to help:

- The next time you want a lift somewhere, think first. Can you walk, ride your bike or take public transportation instead?

- Don't keep your ride waiting while you hunt for your books or have a last-minute chat with a friend. An idling car or school bus wastes gas and pollutes the air.

- Don't ask your driver to "step on it" to get you places faster. A speeding car uses more gas than one that drives at slower speeds.
- Write to your local and federal governments and tell them you want them to support trains, subways and rapid-transit lines, rather than building more roads and freeways. (Some countries are putting their transportation money into high-speed trains that can go up to 200 kph/125mph.)
- On days when you and your friends go to lessons, games or meetings, organize a car pool so fewer cars are used. Your parents will be more than happy not to have to drive so often.

Where Does Energy Come From? / 25

Water Power

The energy produced by falling water is one of the oldest sources of power. Many years ago, people built water wheels on fast-flowing rivers. The wheel had blades attached to it, and when the rushing water passed through the wheel, it would push the blades and make the wheel turn. The wheel could turn heavy stones to grind grain, or turn a saw to cut logs.

People eventually realized that instead of just passing through the blades of a small wheel, a large amount of water could be funneled through pipes and pushed against the blades of a turbine with great force, to work a generator.

There are many advantages to water power, which is called hydro-electric power. Water is free, it doesn't run out like oil or coal, and it seems to be a very simple way to produce energy. Running water itself turns the blades of the turbine, unlike other forms of energy where the energy source is used to heat water to create steam, which then turns the turbines. Water power also appears to be safe and clean, and it doesn't pollute the air or cause acid rain.

But water power has problems, too. A great deal of force is needed to drive turbines big enough to provide power to many homes and factories. Huge dams must be built. These concrete barriers are placed across rivers to hold the water back and create lots of pressure.

Most of the best natural hydro-electric sites in the world already have dams on them. So to meet the demand for more power, governments and power companies are building dams on more remote or smaller rivers, even if the power has to be carried long distances to the places where it will

be used, and even if larger and larger areas must be flooded to create the necessary water pressure.

These new dams are very expensive to build. Roads and airports have to be built, often in wilderness areas, to bring workers and giant machines to the dam site. The dams change the natural landscape immediately around them, and very far downstream. Fish can no longer swim upriver to lay their eggs. When the dam stops the flow of the water, lakes downstream can be turned into giant mud puddles, killing the fish and wildlife that live there. Farmlands and valleys are often flooded, river banks are worn away, and the nests of water birds are drowned. In winter, the release of warm water (that is heated up a bit when it runs through the turbines) can make the ice less solid,

Megadams
All over the world, hydro-electric projects are getting bigger and bigger. In northern Canada the James Bay Project will increase the flow of some rivers by cutting off the flow of others. Huge areas of wilderness will be affected, and no one knows for certain how harmful the project will be to the land, wildlife or people of the region. And in China there are plans to build a $15 billion dam across the Yangtze, the world's third-largest river. The dam will be 6.5 kilometers (4 miles) long and 180 meters (575 feet) high, and its builders claim it will allow the country to develop its industries and become richer. However, a great deal of farmland would be flooded, and over one million people would have to leave their homes.

preventing local people from using the rivers and lakes as ice roads.

Dams can even cause pollution. When the water flow is stopped, the natural cleaning process of the river is stopped, and silt builds up. Sometimes the surrounding forests are flooded, and the trees and underbrush rot. This can cause mercury, a highly dangerous metal, to leak out of the surrounding rocks and soil into the water, poisoning the fish and the people and animals that eat the fish.

So although water power doesn't pollute the air like oil or coal, building more and more hydro-electric stations can seriously harm the earth and the people and animals that depend on the land for their food and shelter.

Where Does Energy Come From? / **29**

Nuclear Power

About fifty years ago, the world was introduced to a new kind of energy—atomic or nuclear energy. Scientists discovered how to split uranium atoms (atoms are the tiniest bits of matter that make up everything on earth) to create very high heat. This heat could be used to boil water and create steam. The force of this steam could turn huge turbines and produce electricity in a nuclear power plant.

At first many people thought that nuclear power would be the answer to all our energy problems. Nuclear power doesn't rely on the disappearing supplies of fossil fuels, and it doesn't cause acid rain, smog or the Greenhouse Effect. It doesn't flood large areas of land. Nuclear power seemed to be a cheaper way to get electricity than using oil or hydro-electric power, and it used uranium, a fuel that some countries have large supplies of. Besides, you don't need a lot of uranium to fuel a power plant. A chunk smaller than a golf ball can produce as much energy as burning twenty railway cars full of coal.

But after a while, more and more people began to realize that there were serious problems with nuclear power.

Nuclear fuel is very radioactive, which means that it produces radiation, an invisible pollution that can make people very sick, even many years after they are exposed to it.

Once most of the uranium atoms have been split, the fuel rods that hold the uranium can't be used to make power anymore, but they still contain enough radioactivity to be dangerous to people for thousands of years. These fuel rods are so deadly that they must be handled by robots. If you stood next to a used fuel rod, fresh out of a reactor, you would receive a lethal dose of radiation in less than twenty seconds.

So far, these used rods have been kept in deep pools of water at the nuclear power plants, but these pools will soon be full. The rods will then have to be stored somewhere far away from people.

Right now, the only proposal is to bury this radioactive garbage in a strong container deep in the earth. The burial sites would have to be protected by guards. It would be very expensive to dig holes that are deep enough and make containers that are strong enough to hold our growing piles of nuclear waste. As well, nobody knows whether groundwater could eventually wear down the containers and carry radioactive waste into wells, lakes and rivers, or whether earthquakes might disturb the burial site.

Uranium fuel rods aren't the only nuclear wastes. When the uranium is taken out of the ground and crushed, most of the radioactive material is left near the mines, where it can contaminate rivers and lakes, as well as the air and soil.

Not only that, but the reactors themselves—the tanks that contain the fuel rods—are radioactive

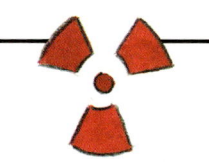

Radiation

Radiation is the term used to describe rays of tiny high-speed particles that shoot out from many different sources—both natural and artificial. The sun, minerals in the earth, x-rays, light, radio and radar waves all produce different kinds of radiation. When radiation is released, the process is called radioactivity.

Some radiation rays are harmless, but split uranium atoms release rays that are very powerful—powerful enough to penetrate a block of concrete 1 meter (3 feet) thick. Even small amounts of these rays can damage or destroy living tissue, causing cancer, radiation sickness and even death.

DO NOT DIG HERE!

If we bury nuclear waste, how can we make sure that future generations won't dig it up? Nuclear waste can be poisonous for many thousands of years, and even our great-great-great-great-grandchildren won't be around to tell people how dangerous it is. After all, archeologists today are still trying to figure out what the ancient Egyptians were thinking of when they built the pyramids over three thousand years ago. Thousands of years from now, people will probably be just as puzzled by our actions. They might not even speak the same languages we do!

Some people think we should build monuments on top of the buried waste. These monuments would have to be very large and very strong and perhaps arranged in a weird pattern to make them look so special that nobody would take them down. The markers would have messages carved on them in several languages and in pictures, warning people not to dig underneath.

If you came across a strange, very old marker that said, "Do not dig here," what would you do?

Write to your utility company, nuclear energy commission and the government leader who is responsible for energy (ask your teacher, parents or librarian to help you find the correct names and addresses). Ask them what they plan to do if there is a nuclear accident, how they are dealing with nuclear waste, and what will happen to the nuclear power plants when it is time to close them down.

inside, and after forty years or so they get worn out and have to be replaced. These dead reactors could be covered with concrete (although the concrete would crumble away long before the reactors were no longer dangerous), or be taken apart by robots and carried some place to be buried. Shutting down a reactor can take several years, and cost $1 billion.

Even if we could be sure that the radioactive waste would stay safely buried until it is no longer harmful, we still have to get this dangerous material to the waste site, perhaps in a ship, or in trucks that pass through towns and cities.

And where should we put these nuclear dumps? Would you want one near your home? Would you want it anywhere near plants or wildlife?

There is another problem. When a nuclear generator is working, radioactive gases are produced. Small amounts leak into the air and water around the generator. There isn't enough radiation to be harmful immediately, but some experts now think that people who live near nuclear power plants or work in them may one day get cancer from the radiation that has built up in their bodies over many years.

Finally, there have been accidents in these reactors. Although the people who run them and build them do everything they can to make them safe, using the most up-to-date equipment, things can go wrong. The computers that are programmed to spot problems are very complicated, and sometimes their messages can be misunderstood. If this happens, the uranium, and eventually the reactor itself, can melt, releasing large amounts of radiation.

Funeral Procession for a Nuclear Reactor

When one nuclear power station was taken apart in Pennsylvania, the reactor was loaded on a barge, carried down the Ohio and Mississippi rivers, through the Panama Canal, up the Pacific coast and along the Columbia River to a nuclear waste dump, where it was eventually buried two storeys underground. The barge traveled 12,700 kilometers (7,900 miles), and took the reactor past cities, towns, beaches and wildlife areas. Smaller parts were loaded on trains and trucks and carted across the United States to the burial site.

In 1979 there was an accident at the Three Mile Island nuclear reactor in the United States. The cooling water in and around the hot reactor accidentally gushed out, letting the temperature of the reactor climb to 2,760 degrees C (5,000 degrees F). Part of the reactor melted and, although not much radiation was released, it took over ten years and $1 billion to clean it up.

The worst nuclear accident occurred at the Chernobyl Nuclear Power Plant in the Soviet Union in 1986, when an explosion blasted radioactive material 1.3 kilometers (4,000 feet) into the air. Almost 200,000 people had to leave their homes, and over 500,000 people were affected by the radiation. Houses and buildings had to be hosed down to wash away as much radioactivity as possible. Contaminated soil had to be scraped off huge areas of land, stored in metal drums and buried as nuclear waste. The wind carried radioactive fallout as far as Italy and Sweden, and sheep in some parts of England became too poisonous to eat. Thirty-two people have already died, but nobody knows how many thousands of others will eventually get cancer or other diseases because of this accident, or what will happen to the plants, forests, lakes and animals that were covered by the leaked radiation.

In spite of these problems, many people still think that nuclear energy is a good thing. They say too much fuss is made about the dangers of radiation. Some governments even think it's okay to pour small amounts of radioactive material down the drain or dump it in the ocean or in the garbage. Besides, they point out, we *need* the energy that nuclear reactors produce. We have no choice but to keep building these power plants, even if nuclear power is risky.

Others say that if we used energy more wisely, we wouldn't need new nuclear power plants. They say that nuclear energy is actually a lot more expensive than we think because of the enormous cost of building and operating the plants safely, getting rid of the waste and taking the used stations apart. And, radiation is still a big problem. Radiation isn't like smog or soot—you can't see it or smell it—but it can be very powerful, and very dangerous.

The world has not been using nuclear power for very long, and there is still a lot that we don't know about it. What will radiation do to people who grow up near nuclear power plants or who work in uranium mines for several years? How badly will a big reactor accident harm people, plants and wildlife? How will we deal with nuclear waste over a long period of time? And what will we do with the hundreds of nuclear power plants in the world, when it comes time to close them down?

Did You Know?
Recycling one aluminum pop can saves the same amount of energy that it takes to run a television for three hours.

Did You Know?

The hairs on a polar bear are hollow, and they aren't really white. They are actually clear, but appear white because they reflect so much light. The clear, hollow hairs carry the sun's energy to the bear's skin to keep the animal warm.

Polar bear fur is one of the most efficient collectors of solar energy known to science. Scientists are now trying to imitate the structure of polar bear fur in solar panels to help collect more of the sun's energy.

Other Sources of Energy

Right now, most of our energy comes from oil, coal, water or nuclear power. But there are other sources of energy as well.

Solar Power

The earth's natural energy comes from the sun. Without the sun's rays, plants wouldn't grow, and animals and people would have no food. When the sun heats the earth, the air moves, causing winds, and water evaporates and falls again as rain, filling our lakes and oceans, and making our rivers run. You could even say that we burn "stored sunlight" when we burn wood and fossil fuels such as oil and coal, which are made of sun-grown plants and animals.

The sun's energy is called solar energy. In one day the amount of solar energy streaming towards the earth equals the energy that could be produced by burning 550 billion tons of coal.

But the sun's energy is spread out over the whole surface of the earth. Most of it hits the oceans, or places where no people live.

It makes sense to use this huge amount of free, safe, clean energy. But if the sun's rays are to be used as a source of power, they must first be collected and concentrated to produce enough heat to boil water. The boiling water will then produce steam that can be used to drive a turbine and run a generator.

Solar power is not a new idea. Almost one hundred years ago, a solar collector was made out of hundreds of small mirrors that collected the sun's rays to boil water. The steam from the hot water was then used to drive an engine. This collector worked, but it weighed 3,600 kilograms (8,000 pounds), and it was too expensive and awkward to make a lot of power.

Since then engineers have been developing new ways to collect the energy from the sun. They have made better solar panels to collect sunlight and convert it into heat. They have invented solar cells that can change sunlight directly into electricity. So far, these cells are too expensive to be used in many everyday items except for small things like calculators, radios and flashlights. But they are used to supply electricity in faraway spots where solar power is still cheaper than running in an electric cable or flying in huge amounts of fuel.

There are already solar power plants in Japan, France, California, Italy and Spain. In California, at the largest solar generator in the world, 1,800

Curtain Power

You can use solar energy in your own house, and it won't cost you a penny. In the winter, simply open the curtains on sunny days to let the sun stream in; in the summer, close the curtains during the day to keep the cool air in. On cool nights, close the curtains to help keep the heat in the house. If your house needs new curtains, help your parents by finding out which kinds of material work better as insulation.

In 1990, cars from all over the world took part in an unusual race in Australia. Forty different cars raced 3,000 kilometers (1,860 miles) across the Australian countryside. All of the cars were powered only by solar energy. The average speed was 60 kph (40 mph), and the winning car finished the race in five days. The Swiss car won, and its manufacturer now has plans to sell solar cars as commuter vehicles within the next five years.

giant mirrors cover about 40 hectares (100 acres). The mirrors are controlled by a computer so they always face the sun, and they reflect sunlight to a boiler on top of a steel tower. The boiler boils water, and the steam drives a generator on the ground. Huge tanks full of crushed rock and oil store the heat so that the generator can operate for seven hours even when the sun isn't shining. This generator creates enough electricity to run 10,000 home air-conditioners, or heat 2,000 to 3,000 homes.

Engineers are also working on other uses for solar energy—sun-powered airplanes, sun-powered boats, sun-powered and sun-heated homes. Many houses now are being built so that their windows face the sun during the brightest times of the day, and some new houses have special panels to collect the sun's warmth.

We must still find out how to change more of the sun's energy into electricity. We must also learn how to store this electricity so power can be

used when the sun doesn't shine, and how to carry the sun-generated electricity through wires over long distances without losing too much power.

But it is only a matter of time before scientists will figure out how to do these things. All they need is money, and public and government support. In the meantime, there are plenty of ways that we can use solar power on a smaller scale—to heat water in our homes, for instance, or provide electricity to a community or subdivision.

Wind Power
You have probably seen pictures of old-fashioned windmills—perhaps a pretty wooden Dutch windmill with cloth sails, or a metal wheel with blades mounted on a tower. When the passing winds push against the sails or blades to make them turn, the movement can be used to pump water out of the ground.

These old pump windmills have been used all over the world for hundreds of years. But engineers are now working on modern windmills that can make electricity. These windmills are made of strong, space-age materials and have sleek designs. Some of them look like giant eggbeaters. One design consists of huge sails mounted on wheeled carts. The wind would push these carts around an oval track, and the wheels would drive a generator powerful enough to provide electricity to a city of 80,000 people.

The good thing about wind power is that it is clean and doesn't pollute the air, the earth or the water. The problem, of course, is that the wind doesn't blow all the time. So on calm days, a windmill doesn't turn.

Although wind power may not be able to be

> **Did You Know?**
> An electric kettle uses half the energy that it takes to heat water on the stove.
>
>

used everywhere, in wide open areas where the winds are strong, it can supply enough power to reduce the load on oil- or gas-fueled generators. In California, for example, where the winds are fairly constant, there are "wind farms." Several windmills are erected near each other on large fields. Together they can create enough electricity to power an entire city.

There are many places in the world where clean wind power could be used instead of polluting fuels. In the meantime, don't forget that wind energy can be used in simple ways as well. Houses and buildings can be designed so that open windows and vents can provide natural cooling.

VOLCANO POWER

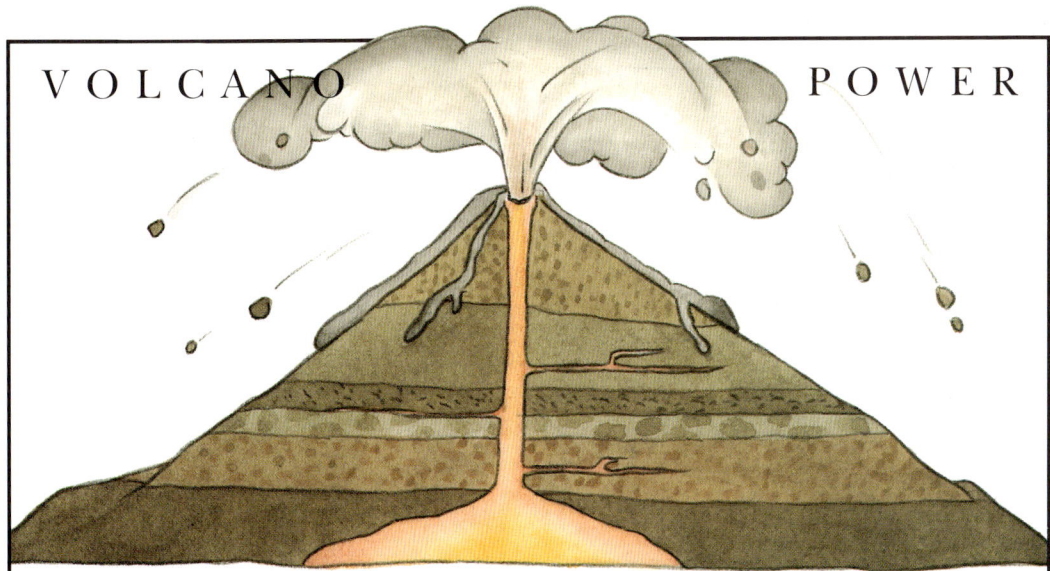

Deep under the earth, there is a layer of very hot, liquid rock called magma. In some places in the world, the magma bubbles up close to the earth's surface, and this underground heat can be used to make geothermal power (*geo* means earth; *thermal* means heat).

Geothermal power plants have been built in the Soviet Union, New Zealand, Italy, Japan, Chile and Hawaii. Deep holes are drilled down to underground pockets of hot water, and the steam that spurts out is fed into turbines to produce electricity.

You can imagine how expensive and difficult it is to drill so far down into the earth. Even if we dig very deep, there are not too many places in the world where the hot water comes close to the earth's surface. Some of these spots are not easy to get at. Others are in the middle of precious wilderness areas, or are too far away from large numbers of people.

There are other problems, too. Geothermal wells release the same gases into the air that cause acid rain. Also, no one really knows what taking so much fluid out of the earth will do to the surrounding area. It could even trigger earthquakes or cause the nearby land to sink.

Finally, the geothermal steam that comes out of the earth is very salty, as well as being polluted with metals that have come out of the underground rock. This water will harm crops and plants if it is allowed to drain away into the land. Some geothermal plants pump the polluted water back into the earth to be reheated, so it doesn't drain into the soil and groundwater, but this isn't always done.

Where Does Energy Come From?

PART 3

What Can We Do?

The message is pretty clear.

The production of energy is creating huge amounts of pollution. We are running out of fossil fuels. New hydro-electric power plants are harming the land. Nuclear power plants are using and producing a deadly poison that we don't know how to get rid of. And the clean and safe energy sources like the sun and wind aren't yet cheap and efficient enough to be used by most people or businesses.

It seems that there is no perfect energy source—one that is unlimited, safe, clean and cheap.

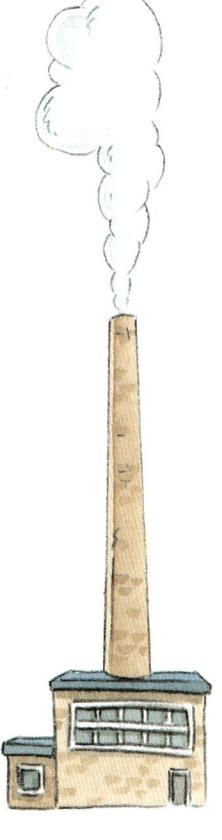

But some experts say that we must keep looking for oil, that we must build more nuclear power plants and bigger hydro-electric dams, because every year we use more energy. Our factories and machines are getting bigger and faster and more powerful. Our homes are filling up with shiny new appliances, electrical equipment and gadgets to do our work for us, make us comfortable, and provide our entertainment. And every year there are more cars on the road, using up more gas and oil.

We are using more and more energy every year, and are doing more and more harm to the earth by doing so.

So what can we *do*?

1) We must stop using so much energy.

Of course, nobody really *wants* to do this. Using as much energy as we want, without having to think about it, is everybody's dream. But a time will come—perhaps by the time you're ready to drive a car—when we will be forced to stop using so much.

Can you imagine if all the gas stations in town closed, you were only allowed to drive your car on certain days, or it was against the law to drive a car with fewer than two passengers in it? What would it be like if outdoor Christmas lights were banned, if stores were only open until noon every day, and you were only allowed to run your washer and dryer or dishwasher at night, when fewer businesses and people were using the available power?

Many of these things have already happened in parts of the world during times when there have been energy shortages. Some are happening right now. Others may happen when more people realize that we are making our planet unlivable by using so many polluting fuels.

You probably think that using less energy will be a real drag. It will be nothing but a nuisance to have to stop and think every time you want to flick a switch or get into a car or plug in another machine or gadget. Maybe you think it is just too depressing to have to think about oil spills every time you fill up at a gas station, or about radiation poisoning every time you turn on the TV, knowing that your electricity comes from a nuclear power station.

But look at it another way. If you don't start using less energy, the world you will live in as a grownup will be far more miserable than living with a bit of inconvenience now. By saving energy today, you are protecting your environment from further pollution.

Be a Draft Detective
Did you know that the average home loses one-quarter of its heat through air leaks?

Find out where the air leaks are in your house. Take a feather, light ribbon, tissue or plastic sandwich bag. Hold the feather near the bottom of each door or window in your house. If the feather moves, cold outdoor air is sneaking into your house. Make a draft stopper for the leaking window or door.

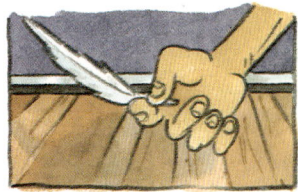

Double-Stocking Draft Stopper
Cut the legs off a pair of old tights. Carefully line one leg with the other, so you have a double thickness. Stuff the leg with dried beans or uncooked rice. Secure the open end tightly with an elastic band. If you like, sew button eyes and a forked tongue onto one end to make a snake face. Place the draft stopper along the bottom of a leaky door or window.

What Can We Do? / 43

So you're really doing yourself a favor by saving energy.

Besides, some of the solutions are very simple. It may take a while to get used to doing these things, but soon you won't even have to think about them.

Around the House
- Don't leave the lights on when there is no one in the room. Turn out the bedroom and bathroom lights before you go down to breakfast in the morning. Turn out the lights if you're the last person out of the house or classroom.
- Don't use reading lights in the daytime unless you have to. Read beside a window instead.
- If you use a dishwasher, make sure it's full before you turn it on. And don't use the Dry cycle. It's the one that uses most of the power.
- In the summer, offer to hang clothes outside instead of using the dryer. Your clothes will last longer and smell great.
- Turn off the TV and stereo when no one is watching or listening to them.
- Don't leave the door to your house open in the winter. Keep the warm air in.
- Turn down the heat on your thermostat, especially at night. Wear slippers and an extra sweatshirt. Keep a blanket on your couch to snuggle into while you're watching TV or reading.
- Don't use air-conditioning if you don't have to. Sleep in the basement on hot nights.

Out and About

- Write to businesses that you see wasting energy—office buildings that leave all their lights on overnight, buildings that are over-heated or over-air-conditioned, companies that put too much energy-wasting packaging on their products.

- Buy things made of recycled paper, glass, aluminum or plastic. It takes less energy to make these things from recycled material than to make them from scratch.

- Whenever you can, buy things in reusable containers—the kind you can take back to the store so they can be filled again.

- Before you buy something, ask yourself questions. Is it made of something that is scarce? Was a lot of energy used when it was made? Can it be recycled? Could I do without it, or buy something that is less damaging to the environment instead?

What Can We Do? / **45**

2) We must start using energy more efficiently.

Using energy efficiently means getting the most out of the energy that we do use. Many power companies, for example, are planning to reuse the hot water that makes the steam that runs the generator. This hot water can be recycled to heat homes and buildings near the power station.

There are many ways you can use energy more efficiently. It isn't hard, but it may take a little planning and thinking:

- After you have a bath, leave the hot water in the tub for awhile. The warm water will help heat the room.

- Don't leave the stove on unnecessarily. Using a microwave oven to reheat a bowl of soup uses less than half the energy you would use keeping the soup warm on the stove.

- Think before you plug in an appliance. If you are making a piece of toast for yourself in the morning, make one for someone else in the family, too, so you just use the toaster once.

- Before driving to a game, ask whether you can pick up a friend or two on the way, so you use just one car. Even better, take the bus or your bike. Or walk.

- Move furniture that is blocking warm air ducts in your house. Don't throw your clothes or books on top of heat ducts.

These days, there are many new inventions that can help us save energy. They do the same job as the old versions, but they do it more efficiently. There are new lightbulbs that use less energy than regular lightbulbs. There are furnaces, fridges, stoves, washers and dryers that are designed to use less energy. There are insulating blankets that you can wrap around your water heater to save energy. There are timers that turn off your lights or turn down your thermostat for you. There are new super-windows that you can put on your house to keep more of the cold air out and the hot air in. And there are cars that go farther on a tankful of gas, and that are designed to put fewer harmful gases into the air.

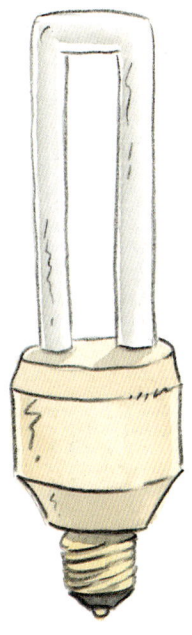

Of course, driving an energy-efficient car won't do much good if more and more people drive more and more cars. Using energy-efficient devices doesn't mean we can still use all the energy we want. But it can make a difference—a big difference—in the amount of energy we use.

3) We must start using alternative energy sources.

Some people say that solar energy and wind energy are still too awkward and expensive to be used on a large scale. But that's not the whole story. Every year, governments give the oil, hydro-electric and nuclear industries billions of dollars to help them find more oil, build bigger dams and construct new reactors. If the companies developing wind and solar energy got even a fraction of this money, they could go a long way toward solving many of our energy problems.

There are also people who say that using oil, for example, is much cheaper than getting electricity from a solar generator. But would it really be cheaper if each one of us had to pay our share of

cleaning up all the oil spills that occur in the world every year?

We must support the companies that are developing clean forms of energy. If we encourage our governments to give them money, they will find ways to make these things work.

There are many scientists and engineers who are working hard to find new and better ways of providing the world with energy that is safe, plentiful, cheap and doesn't harm the earth. Here are just some of the ideas they are working on:

- using the energy stored in sound waves to make electricity;
- using magnets to move high-speed trains or make electrical power;
- using holograms and mirrors to aim sunlight into rooms without windows;
- turning sewage sludge into oil;
- using animal and plant waste as fuel.

Other engineers are working on generators that use the movement of the ocean's tides or waves to make power, cars that don't run on gasoline, huge

airships that could replace some gas-guzzling airplanes, or rapid-transit systems that are so fast and efficient that they could replace many private automobiles.

Some of these ideas may not become practical for many years. Others need only money, a little time and public support.

There are ways you can help:

- Write to your town council and ask them what they are doing to encourage people to ride bikes and buses instead of driving cars. Tell them you want more bus lanes and special bike paths in your town or city.
- Ask your government leaders what they are doing to encourage people to use alternative energy sources. Tell them you would like to see more money given to groups that are developing solar and wind energy.
- Write to your local newspaper and tell them you'd like to see more articles on energy and pollution issues.
- Ask your science teacher to invite a solar energy expert to visit your school.

What Can We Do? / **49**

4) We must find out more about the energy we use — where it comes from, and how we use it.

Do you know how your home is heated? How far your car can go on a tankful of gas? Where your closest nuclear power station is? Where your electricity comes from?

Energy is one of the most important issues facing us right now. It will continue to be important in the future. You might want to find out more about careers in the energy field, or perhaps you can do your next science fair project on energy.

And remember that you live in just one country. All over the world, more babies are born every year, and people are living longer. This means more people using more energy. Some countries are just starting to use lots of energy, so that they, too, can build hospitals and factories and grow enough food to feed their growing populations.

You Can Make a Difference

Can a bunch of kids turning out the lights and walking to school and washing their own dishes really make a difference to such a big problem like energy?

In fact, we use so much energy, that if everyone took even a few small steps, it would make an enormous difference.

- If all homes and businesses in North America used energy-efficient furnaces, we would not need the Trans-Alaska Pipeline—the pipeline that supplied the oil that the *Exxon Valdez* spilled into the ocean.
- If we all drove energy-efficient cars, insulated our homes, used efficient furnaces and took public transportation as often as we could, we could save more oil than we will ever find under the earth.
- If all businesses in the Canadian province of Ontario used energy-efficient lighting, we could close down two large nuclear reactors or four coal-burning generators.

How Many Times a Day Do You Open Your Fridge?

To find out, make a chart and tape it to the front of your fridge, along with a pencil. Ask each member of your family to mark the chart whenever they open the fridge. Add up the check marks at the end of the day. See how your result compares with the average household (22 times).

Every time you open your refrigerator, the cold air falls out, so the refrigerator has to use more energy to keep itself cool. Think about what you want before you open the fridge. If you keep leftovers in containers that all look the same, help out by making labels for the containers and organizing them so you know exactly where stuff is.

What Can We Do?

All Cars Eat Gas

How much carbon dioxide does a running car engine release into the air? One high school teacher explained it this way: A car that drives 10 kilometers (6 miles) produces a refrigerator-sized blob of carbon dioxide. It would take more than a gymnasium full of clean air to dilute this carbon dioxide to safe levels. In other words, every time you drive 10 kilometers (6 miles), you are using up more than the amount of air that is contained in the average school gym.

Do you know how often you drive 10 kilometers? How far is it from your home to your school? Your shopping center? Your hockey arena?

- If every American used a car that got one more mile per gallon, we could save 500,000 barrels of oil a day.
- If every person who used electricity replaced one lightbulb with an energy-efficient compact fluorescent lightbulb, fifty of the world's large nuclear power plants could be shut down.

The world needs more scientists and engineers who will work to develop clean energy sources. It needs politicians and company presidents and teachers and parents who care about a clean earth.

And it needs kids who are prepared to use and have a little less so that everyone can have enough. We have to change our habits, find out what's going on, and start making a fuss to the people who are making decisions about energy.

Each one of us can make a small difference. Together, we can do a lot.

GLOSSARY

Acid rain: Rain that has been made acidic by gases from car exhaust and factories and power plants that burn fossil fuels.

Atom: The smallest particle of matter. There are millions of atoms in a grain of salt and billions in a drop of water.

Battery: A container holding special chemicals that store small amounts of electricity.

Carbon dioxide: A gas that is a natural part of the atmosphere. Too much carbon dioxide in the air causes the Greenhouse Effect, trapping the sun's heat in the earth's atmosphere.

Coal: A solid black fossil fuel made of ancient decomposed plants.

Cogeneration: Reusing waste power a second time, as when the leftover hot water from a power plant is used to heat nearby homes and buildings.

Fission: The splitting of atoms to generate heat. So far, only uranium atoms can be split.

Gasoline: A fuel used in automobile engines and made from oil (petroleum) or natural gas.

Generator: A machine that changes energy into electricity.

Geothermal power: Power made from the heat of the earth's crust.

Greenhouse Effect: The warming of the earth's atmosphere caused by gases such as carbon dioxide, which trap the sun's heat and cause the temperature at the earth's surface to increase.

Hydro-electric station: A power station that makes electricity from the energy of falling water.

Meltdown: The accident that occurs when a nuclear reactor overheats, and part or all of the fuel turns into liquid and collapses.

Methane: A natural gas that can be burned as fuel.

Natural gas: A fossil fuel made of ancient buried plants and animals. Gas comes out of the earth's crust through natural openings or drilled wells.

Nitrogen oxide: A gas formed when fossil fuels are burned. Nitrogen oxide contributes to acid rain.

Nuclear energy: The energy created by splitting uranium atoms.

Nuclear radiation: Rays of tiny particles that are released when uranium atoms are split.

Nuclear reactor: A tank containing the uranium atoms that are split to create heat.

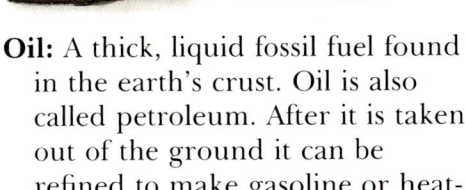

Oil: A thick, liquid fossil fuel found in the earth's crust. Oil is also called petroleum. After it is taken out of the ground it can be refined to make gasoline or heating oil.

Propane: A natural gas that can be used as fuel.

Scrubbers: Devices that can be used in smokestacks to help clean up the smoke.

Smog: Polluted fog caused by car and factory exhaust gases when they are hit by sunlight.

Solar power: Collecting and using the heat from the sun.

Sulfur dioxide: A gas formed when fossil fuels are burned. Sulfur dioxide contributes to acid rain.

Turbine: A machine that is run by the energy of steam, gases or falling water.

Uranium: A radioactive metal that is used as a fuel in nuclear reactors.

INDEX

Acid rain, 17, 18-19, 22, 24, 25, 26, 30, 41, 54 (glossary)
Animal waste as fuel, 17, 48
Antarctica, 17
Atom, 30, 31, 54 (glossary)
Atomic power. See Nuclear power.
Automobile, 12, 17, 22, 23, 25, 47, 48, 49, 50, 51, 52. See also Electric car, Gasoline.

Battery, 54 (glossary)
Blackout. See Power blackout.

Cancer, 33, 34
Car. See Automobile.
Carbon dioxide, 17, 18, 20, 22, 52, 54 (glossary). See also Greenhouse Effect.
Chernobyl, 34
Coal, 12, 13, 14, 17 18-20, 26, 29, 30, 36, 37, 51, 54 (glossary)
Cogeneration, 46, 54 (glossary)
Computers, 10, 33

Draft stopper, 43

Earthquakes, 31, 41
Efficiency, 44-47, 51-52
Electric car, 23
Electricity, 5, 13-14, 30, 37, 38-39, 40, 41, 47, 48, 50
Exxon Valdez, 20-21, 51

Fission, 54 (glossary)
Flooding, 28, 29, 30
Fossil fuels, 12, 13, 14-25, 30, 36, 42
Fuel rods, 31

Gas. See Natural gas.
Gasoline, 12, 14-15, 22, 23, 25, 43, 47, 48, 49, 54 (glossary)
Generator, 5, 13-14, 26, 37, 38, 39, 40, 54 (glossary)

Geothermal power, 41, 54 (glossary)
Global warming. See Greenhouse Effect.
Greenhouse Effect, 17, 20, 22, 25, 30, 50, 54 (glossary)

Holograms, 48
Hydro-electric power. See Water power.

James Bay Project, 29

Lightbulbs, 47, 51

Magma, 41
Magnets, 48
Meltdown, 33, 34, 54 (glossary)
Mercury, 29
Methane, 17, 23, 55 (glossary)
Microwave, 46
Mirrors, 48

Natural gas, 12, 13, 14, 17-18, 19, 23, 40, 55 (glossary)
Nitrogen oxide, 18, 54 (glossary)
Nuclear power, 30-35, 42, 47, 55 (glossary)
Nuclear reactor, 31-33, 34, 35, 50, 51, 52, 55 (glossary)
Nuclear waste, 31, 32, 33, 34

Oil, 12, 13, 14-22, 25, 26, 29, 36, 40, 42, 47, 52, 55 (glossary). See also Gasoline.
Oil spills, 20-21, 48, 51

Packaging, 45
Petroleum. See Oil.
Plant waste as fuel, 17, 48
Polar bear fur, 36
Pollution, 11, 18-25, 29, 30, 41, 42, 52. See also Acid rain, Carbon dioxide, Oil spills.
Power blackout, 10-11
Propane, 23, 55 (glossary)

Radiation, 30, 31, 33, 34, 35, 55 (glossary)
Radioactivity, 30, 31, 32, 33, 34, 35
Recycling, 35, 45

Scrubbers, 18-19, 55 (glossary)
Smog, 17, 22, 30, 55 (glossary)
Solar cells, 37
Solar panels, 37
Solar power, 36-39, 42, 47, 49, 55 (glossary)
Sound waves, 48
Sulfur dioxide, 17, 18, 19, 55 (glossary)
Sun. See Solar power.
Supertankers. See Oil spills.

Three Mile Island, 34
Tidal power, 48
Tires as fuel, 14
Trans-Alaska Pipeline, 51
Trees, 22, 24
Turbine, 13-14, 26, 28, 30, 37, 41, 55 (glossary)
TV, 11, 35

Uranium, 30, 31, 33, 55 (glossary)

Volcano power, 41

Water power, 12, 13, 26-29, 30, 42, 47
Windmills, 39, 40
Wind power, 39-40, 42, 47
Wood, 12, 22, 36

Yangtze River Project, 29